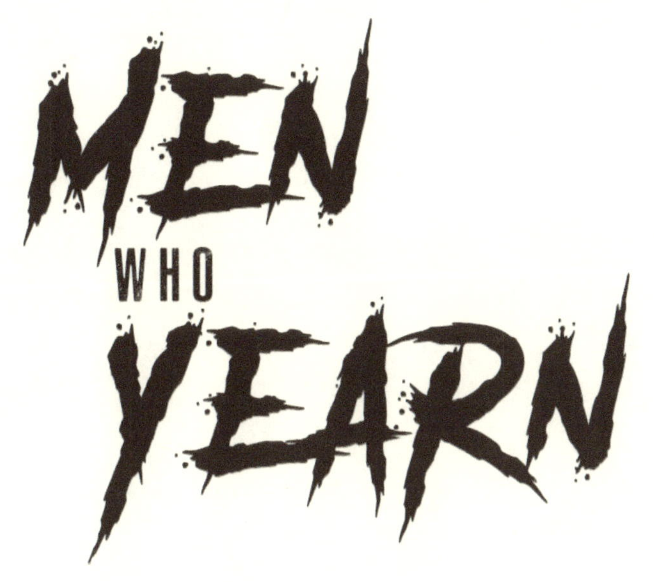

MEN WHO YEARN

CLARISSA WILD

DESCRIPTION

For years he watched.

Diligently.

Dutifully.

Starving for her touch.

Never once did he cross the line...

Until she made him beg.

**MEN WHO YEARN is a dark romance
prelude SHORT STORY to BOYS WHO HUNT.
Contains disturbing content that might not be
suitable for all readers.**

ONE

Year 4 – Spine Ridge University

Every bite I take out of my sandwich becomes harder and harder to swallow because of those eyes. Those damn dark brown eyes that look up from a laptop every other minute to take a very direct, intense glance at us.

At me.

Or at least, that's what it feels like while I'm sitting

here in the grass, trying to enjoy my lunch. It's not often we all get to hang out together as a group. Though, it did take me a while to get used to the fact that Penelope and Crystal are going out with boys from the Skull and Serpent Society and the Tartarus House, where some of the most notorious boys on campus have made their home.

But not even them are as unnerving as the forty-year-old suited-up man with a chiseled jaw and a neatly shaven beard staring at us from a bench in the distance.

"Goddammit …" I murmur to myself, as I take another bite.

"What's wrong?" Penelope asks.

"Nothing," I say, swiftly swallowing it, not wanting to make a fuss when we're finally together again.

Especially not while Felix is sitting across from me.

Because it's most definitely his dad working on that bench.

"So … Felix …" I try to smile but it's only returned with a snarl.

"What?" he growls.

Penelope shoves him with her elbow and it

immediately makes him loose his murderous gaze. "Be nice, please." She looks at me. "Go on. What'd you want to ask him? I promise he won't bite." She chuckles.

"At least not her," Dylan muses, and Felix throws him a deathly glare.

Felix takes a big bite out of his sandwich, and I clear my throat to get rid of the awkward silence. "So, your father is the dean, right?"

"Unfortunately."

"Don't you find it odd? I mean, since he's here every day, talking with other students when they don't even know he's your dad."

He simply shrugs. "I don't care."

"As long as he lets us do whatever we want, why does it matter?" Dylan says, raising a brow.

"He's very strict, even though you can't see it," Penelope says.

I frown. "Really?"

She nods. "He's protective over his kids."

"He actually threatened Lana's boyfriends," Crystal pitches in, and everyone looks at her. "She told me she had a tough time convincing him they were all right."

"Not the least bit surprising to me," Alistair says, folding his arms.

"Those fuckers don't deserve her," Felix says, making a fist.

"Felix, chill. Please." Penelope rolls her eyes. "It's Lana's choice, not yours."

"Well, it's good that your father cares so much about you and Lana," I say, and I glance at him while he types away on his laptop. I wonder what's so important that it couldn't wait until he got back into his office. This must be break-time for him too.

"He's watching us, isn't he?" Felix grumbles.

I tentatively nod. "Can't tell for sure, but I think so."

Felix sighs out loud. "For fuck's sake, he really doesn't have a fucking life."

"What do you mean?" I ask.

"Work means everything for Mr. Rivera," Penelope explains. "It's just … the way he is."

"Bullshit," Felix says. "He just doesn't *have* anything else that's interesting enough."

I tilt my head, brows furrowed. "What do you mean … have?"

"Hobbies. Fun …" Dylan's brows wriggle. "A girlfriend."

Felix rolls up the wrapper of his sandwich and chucks it at Dylan. "Shut the fuck up." But all Dylan does is laugh hysterically.

"It can't be that bad, right?" Crystal asks.

"Oh, it is," Alistair mumbles from the corner, avoiding Felix' gaze as if he's afraid of swift vengeance in the form of a half-finished sandwich smacking into his cheeks.

I take another glance at Mr. Rivera, the sunlight casting an eerie shadow on the pavement beneath him. But when he glances up from his work again, the unease that stirs in my stomach only grows wilder.

***

Days later

I put my laptop on the study desk in the library and

throw my bag on the floor, breathing out a sigh from all the homework I still have to do for the finals. But when I come back up to open up my laptop, there's a guy a few feet away from me that I really don't want to see.

"Motherf…" I mutter to myself as he struts towards me with those hungry eyes. "Johnny, I'm not interested. Give it a fucking rest."

"Girl, let me buy you a drink. Please. Just one drink. One."

I raise a brow and lower my latop screen. "No."

"Oh, c'mon. It's just a drink. Why not?"

"Do you know these two fucking letters? N. O? Learn 'em."

I roll my eyes and open up my latop right in his face so I don't have to look at it anymore.

"Hey." Suddenly, he grips my screen. Too tightly. "I've been nothing but nice to you, and yet you're being nothing but a—"

"A what?" My eyes rise to meet his in disdain. "Say it. Fucking say it … Bitch."

His eyes twitch.

CRACK.

Just the tips of his fingers break through my screen.

Fuck it. Now he's gone and done it.

I punch him in the teeth so hard one of them flies off, and my laptop drops to the floor. But after months of being bothered by this fucker while I'm trying to study, it was fucking worth it to see his face in shambles.

"Fucking bitch!" he growls, trying to punch me back, but I jump off the stool just in time.

The librarian is already screaming at us to stop, and I know she's called the guards, but I can't waste time waiting on help that'll arrive too late.

This fucker deserved that pummel, but he's bigger than I am, and I'm not risking my own goddamn life to win this fight, so I run off through the doors and out into hallways.

"I've got your fucking laptop!" he screams. "Come and get it then, girl!"

He swings it around like a trophy with which he can lure me back to him.

Fuck that guy.

I ram into him with everything I have and manage to tackle him to the ground, punching him with everything I have. He grabs my curly hair and tears at it, spitting in my face, and I shriek from the pain. He grabs my body and rolls me over, slamming me into the wall. I cough and heave from the sudden loss of oxygen in my lungs, but my eyes burst open at the sight of him chucking my own laptop at me.

"Yeah, that's what I thought," Johnny says, spitting on the floor.

Suddenly, two guards jump on top of him and force him to the ground in front of me, while he screams at the top of his lungs, and it almost makes me want to give him another kick just for good measures.

Bystanders are just staring at him instead of helping me, until someone in a suit barges through the crowd and marches straight at me. The dean … Mr. Rivera.

"Miss Pearce, are you all right?" He holds out his hand, but for a second I'm mesmerized by those hauntingly dark eyes boring a hole into my face. Too obsessed to even move.

His eyes twitch as his fingers touch mine, and he

briefly retracts them before he grips my hand firmly and helps me up. I stumble and steady myself, so I don't crash into him.

What is he doing here?

"I heard the ruckus all the way down the hallway while I was speaking with Mrs. Rayborn." His eyes briefly skim over my face and body. "Are you hurt?"

I shake my head and pat down my off-the shoulder orange dress, then pluck at my hair to make sure he didn't rip it out. "I'm fine." I glance sideways past him at Johnny, whose being held back by the guards. His entire face is covered in blood, and his nose is crooked now. Hopefully permanently. "He isn't."

"We're going go to my office," the dean says, and he nods at the guards to follow him. "Bring Mr. Brown."

Under the scrutinizing eyes of my peers, I pick up my broken laptop and tuck it under my arm, as we're both escorted up the stairs. I feel humiliated and can't stop throwing side-eyes at Johnny the moment we're in Mr. Rivera's office. He's snorting up blood from his nose and all they did was offer him a single napkin.

Hope he drowns in his own blood.

The door slams shut and the guards put Johnny in a chair in the corner while I stay put. I'm not taking one step closer in that lunatic's direction.

Mr. Rivera leans against his own desk, arms folded. The guards stay in the room, both sporting a stern look on their faces as they stare down Johnny. One wrong move and he's—

"Mr. Brown. You're expelled."

"What?" Johnny shrieks, still dabbing his nose.

My jaw drops.

"You beat up another student in broad daylight."

"She starte—"

"Fuck you, I didn't do shit," I retort, ready to whoop his ass again. "You destroyed my laptop."

"So what, I've only tried to get you to like me, and all you do is throw it back in my face."

"What don't you understand about 'no'?" I repeat, making a face.

"Enough," Mr. Rivera interjects, rubbing his scruffy, chiseled jaw. "I don't care about your reasonings, Mr. Brown. You're not going to stay for another day."

"That's bullshi—"

Mr. Rivera steps away from the desk in such a menacing manner that it even steals my breath away as he approaches Johnny. He doesn't even have to touch him to make him cower in his seat.

"You hurt Miss. Pearce." His voice darkens. "Apologize."

I swallow away the lump in my throat.

Mr. Rivera grips his chin and forces his head to turn, and he leans in to whisper, "Apologize."

I stare into Johnny's fearful eyes as he mutters, "I'm sorry."

Mr. Rivera releases his face so harshly it almost makes Johnny fall backwards with chair and all.

He walks back to his desk. "How much money did that laptop cost?"

"Um … five hundred? I can't remem—"

"You will give Miss. Pearce a thousand."

"What?!" Johnny gets up.

"Sit down," Mr. Rivera growls, and his guards swiftly place their hands on his shoulders, forcing him to sit. "Either you pay up now, or I will send a letter to your family informing them no member of the Brown family may ever enter Spine Ridge University grounds again."

"That has to be illegal," Johnny mumbles.

Mr. Rivera looks at him from over his shoulder, the darkness in his eyes something to behold. "This is *my* university."

Johnny gulps, and subsequently pulls out a checkbook. "Do you have a pen?"

One of the guards plucks a pencil out of his pockets and Johnny snatches it from his hand, then swiftly scribbles onto the paper and tears it off. "Here." He chucks it my way, but it lands on the floor.

Mr. Rivera grunts with frustration. "Pick. It. Up."

Johnny narrows his eyes at me, bending over to pick it up, which forces him to practically bow to me. He holds out the paper to me, and I take it before he decides he's no longer going to play this game.

"You can grab your things from your dorm and leave," Mr. Rivera says.

"I gave her the money," Johnny answers.

"Was I not clear enough when I said you were expelled?" Mr. Rivera's eyes twitch. "I don't say things I don't mean. Get. Out."

Johnny gets up from his seat, the look on his face filled with rage as he marches past the guards, shoving one of them aside before he opens the door and slams it so harshly behind him the whole room shakes.

Mr. Rivera clears his throat. "Leave us."

I get up.

"Kayla. Stay."

Kayla? He knows my first name?

His guards exit the room, leaving nothing but silence. A deafening, heart-throbbing silence.

When he turns around, light pouring in from the window behind him scatters around his frame, and I can barely look at him without squinting. He's quite tall and handsome with those sharp features of his and those killer eyes that are half-mast, but something about his facial expression gives way for melancholy. Like there is an invisible scar that runs deeper than skin.

"I'm sorry you had to witness that." He swallows,

and I don't know why I focus on his Adam's apple moving the way it does, or his tongue as it briefly swipes his lips.

"He's been quite a nuisance to you, hasn't he?"

I nod. "He's been trying to get in my pants for months now. With no luck, or I wouldn't be sitting here."

"I know."

My eyes narrow. "How, exactly?"

An unhinged lopsided smile forms on his face, and he points at the camera in the corner of the room.

Well, that makes sense. "Oh."

"My guards and I keep an eye on everything that goes around here on campus. For the safety of the students, of course."

"Right. A lot of shady shit happens at this campus. Yet you find time to watch me be harassed and personally come to my help."

He leans back against the desk. "Penelope … is my son's girlfriend. I'm keeping an eye out on her friends, for her sake."

Interesting. I wonder why. "Is Penelope in

trouble?"

"No. Let's just say I'm making sure everyone is safe. That includes Penelope's friends, like you."

I take a deep breath and nod. "Thank you."

He approaches me and places a hand on my shoulder. "If that guy bothers you again, tell me."

He's close. Too close for comfort, because I can feel every inch of every one of his fingers connecting with my skin. "Promise me you will, Kayla."

I can barely collect my thoughts as I inhale a sharp breath. "I promise."

He's not even looking at me and yet this one simple hand on my shoulders has my knees quaking. "Good girl."

TWO

Kayla

I adjust my watch and start the timer before I continue my evening jog across campus during the evening. There aren't a lot of people outside anymore, except for those attending a party at the Tartarus house. Luckily, that's far away from where I'm running.

I like having the peace and quiet around me while I jog, because it helps me focus on the audiobook I'm listening to, and it makes it much easier to keep going.

When I spot a bunch of drunk students headed my way, I veer off-track and go into the direction of the main gates. It wouldn't hurt to jog up and down the mountain road a bit. I won't go all the way down, but it'll have a nice view.

I pause after I've passed the gates to take a breath for a moment and admire my surroundings. Priory Forest is so freaking haunting at night with all those animal sounds, and the leaves rustling in the wind almost makes it look like the trees themselves could come to life at any moment.

Sudden rustling leaves put me on edge, and I turn around to see what it was.

A fox, or a raccoon, maybe?

Two dark eyes appear from behind a tree, and panic swells in my body.

I turn and make a run for it, but a strong hand swiftly wraps around my waist and pulls me back into the forest.

What the f—

I shriek, but his other hand clasps around my mouth, sealing the noise inside.

Adrenaline peaks as I dig my heels into the ground and slam my fists into his grip, to no avail. While tears well up in my eyes, he drags me behind a stone and pulls me close to him.

"Ssstt!" A low voice hisses in my ear, and I stop squealing.

Who is this man?

What is he going to do with me?

Suddenly, more rustles are audible up ahead, and a twig snaps in half.

My breathing is erratic, while his comes in heavy strokes. I can feel it as my body is sandwiched between him and the rock.

What the fuck is going on?

He leans in, hot breath fanning against the rim of my ear. "I'll remove my hand if you promise not to scream."

Sweat drops roll down my back as I nod.

"Don't move. Don't make a sound," he adds, his voice low … almost threatening.

Not wanting to aggravate him further, I agree. It's the best shot I have at getting away from him as soon as possible. He removes his hand, but when I turn to see who it is, my jaw drops and I feel faint.

"Mr. Rivera?"

His dark eyes bore into mine, as if to impale me with a secret I'll be forced to keep or die with.

I swallow down the panic.

What is he doing?

A rock flicks against the stone we're huddled behind.

SNAP!

His hand dives into his pocket and my eyes widen again when he pulls out a gun.

Oh God.

He gets up, and my eyes instinctively close to avoid looking into the barrel as I expect to be shot.

"Stay down," Rivera barks.

BANG!

My body jolts up and down from the sound. Someone groans in pain.

BANG! BANG!

Something makes a thudding sound as it drops to the floor like a sack of potatoes, and it makes my eyes burst open again. I slowly move to peek around the corner of the big stone. Somewhere a few feet away from us, between the trees and on the piles of leaves, lies a body … dripping with blood.

Fuck.

Mr. Rivera tucks his gun away and checks the man on the ground, turning over his floppy body to empty his pockets. All I want to do is make a run for it, but my body feels frozen against this cold stone. Mere seconds ago I thought I was the one who was going to die.

"Who is he?" I ask.

Mr. Rivera looks up at me after he's done inspecting the man. Mr. Rivera wipes his hand on his pants and hisses, sucking in a breath. "Do you want the truth or a lie to soothe your conscience?"

He takes a step closer and I crawl backwards, but he winces in pain and falls to his knees, grunting.

I hold my breath, watching him for a moment.

He shot someone in cold blood right in front of me.

The dean of Spine Ridge University shot someone

in the middle of the night right outside campus. In front of a student.

And it didn't even faze him.

Is he going to kill me next?

Or did he try to protect me?

He lifts up his head and glances at me again before his hand rises from his outer thigh.

Blood cakes his palm.

He can't walk. He's not a threat.

Without thinking, I crawl to him.

"You've been shot," I say.

"I misjudged his aim." He groans again as I help him up. "We have to get out of here. Quick."

I put my arm around his shoulder. "Can you walk?"

He nods. "A little."

"C'mon." I pull him with me towards the open road and all the way up the mountain road until we reach the gates where we pause for a moment. "That fucker slipped right past the guards."

"He was on campus grounds?" I ask, shocked.

"He undercover. The guards didn't notice the logo on his boots, but I did. I lured him out so he wouldn't be able to hurt more students," he answers. "But I didn't anticipate one of them being outside of campus walls."

I rub my lips together, knowing full well he's talking about me.

"Can you take me to my office? I have supplies there."

"What about the nurse' office?" I ask as we head inside the building.

"She's not working tonight, I sent her home to rest after dealing with… a lot, lately." He peeks to the side of the stairs. "There's a staff only elevator in the corner, behind the staircase."

"Good, because I'm not dragging you up these stairs," I say, and we head towards it and step inside.

He holds up his keycard and the door closes, leaving only silence. I look down at his pants which are staining crimson red fast. But when I look back up, he's staring right back at me, and it catches me off-guard.

The doors open and I pull him along with me towards the third door on the third floor, room 333, the dean's office.

We go inside, and I kick the door closed as he struggles to get to his chair, where he takes a breath, and then places his gun on the desk. I stare at the metal that just ended someone's life with ease. The man who pulled the trigger is sitting right across from me.

But am I afraid … or intrigued?

He points at his desk. "There's a first-aid kit in there. Bottom drawer. Can you grab it for me … please?"

The way he says *please* has my knees trembling.

I approach the desk and sift through the drawer until I find what he wants and open it. There's gauze and alcohol pads in there, a few bits and pieces I can use, but not much.

I walk to him and go to my knees in front of him.

"What are you doing?" he mutters.

I look between his legs at the wound protruding through his clothes, but his index finger lifts my chin and forces me to look into his eyes.

God, those eyes. They never manage to break my gaze. They're so bright and yet … deeply haunting.

"I need to look at the wound," I say.

"You don't have to—"

"Let me do this."

I gently nudge his legs open to take a better look.

"I can't put on the gauze like this, Mr. Rivera."

His eyes narrow as I lean forward and grab his belt buckle, and his hand immediately stops me. His eyes home in on me, slowly draping down my body in this dark blue top and leggings, his top teeth drawing in his bottom lip for just a second. But I noticed.

"Call me Salvator."

A shiver runs up and down my spine.

He releases my hand.

I stay frozen for a second, not sure if I should continue or if I'm overstepping.

I am. I know I am.

But this man … I can feel the yearning from miles away, for months on end, and yet … nothing.

Nothing happens because he won't let it happen.

Until tonight.

I swallow away the lump in my throat and gently tug at his zipper and button, pulling it all away so I can peel down his pants slowly just below the wound. But the second it pulls over his ample package, it bobs up and down so much my eyes can't help but zoom in on it.

Good God. He's packing.

Fucking focus, Kayla.

I avert my eyes and grab the kit, dabbing cotton into the alcohol before I bring it to his skin. "This might hurt a little."

I clean up the wound, but it doesn't even seem to faze him. Not an inch of pain mars his face, as though all the suffering has already consumed his soul years ago, and all that's left is a man impervious to agony, except for one… simple … ache.

"I'm sorry you had to witness me kill someone," he says all of the sudden. "I hadn't anticipated anyone being there."

I breathe out a sigh. "I wasn't following you, Mr. Rive—Salvatore. I was just taking a jog."

He grabs my other hand. "I know." A soft smile briefly forms on his face, and it makes my body heat up.

"I'd like to know the truth now," I say. "Why did you kill him?"

He tilts his head. "He was an assassin from the Bones Brotherhood."

"Assassin?" I frown.

"They've been trespassing this campus to hunt my daughter Lana after she got into a fight with them."

I pause after I've put the gauze on his wound.

"Wow."

I didn't know they were involved in this kind of stuff. His daughter, being hunted by a known drug dealing and trafficking gang? No wonder he pulled the trigger on that guy without a second thought. This must be kept off-the books completely.

"I couldn't risk them finding her," he adds, clearing his throat, as I continue tending to his wound.

"I understand."

When I'm done, I put a piece of gauze on top and try to tape it down.

"Suture it." He gazes down at me.

"Don't you want the hospital—"

"I can't risk this going public," he says. "Please."

God. The way this strict-looking, domineering man begs could make a woman want to offer up her entire life on a silver platter.

I nod and grab the needle and thread, then carefully pierce his skin. "This *will* hurt."

"I can take it," he answers, clenching his jaw as I go to work.

I've never seen a man hold his shit together as well as Mr. Rivera does. It's like he must remain in control at all cost, even at the expense of his own sanity … his own life.

"I'm sorry you had to witness me kill someone," he says all of the sudden.

I pause mid-suturing and look up into his hungry eyes and for a second there I almost thought I saw his actual cock bobbing up and down again.

"Are you afraid of me?"

I glance at the gun still lying on the desk.

"No. I've seen plenty of violence. I just never imagined it following me here to this prestige University. I'm not afraid of anything."

I finish up the last sutures.

"But I do know when to keep my mouth shut."

I place the needle and thread back into the kit and place a piece of gauze on top of the sutures, sealing it with a few pieces of tape. But when I attempt to remove my hand, he grabs ahold of it pushes it back down.

The intense gaze in his eyes holds mine like he's commanding the very essence that moves my body.

"I like listening to you talk."

I swallow, and his eyes follow a single bead of sweat as it rolls down from my neckline into the crevice between my breasts, and he licks his lips again, this time much slower, much more pronounced.

As if he wants me to see *it*.

His cock, bouncing up and down, right in front of me.

THREE

He's been watching me for so long.

At first, I thought I was imagining it.

That I was dreaming it up and that all he was doing was watching out for his kids.

But I have never in my life seen a man this ready to beg for a woman on her knees.

With both hands still on his thighs, I lean up until he inches back, his ragged breath clearly audible from up close. His hands release mine as my tits hover close to his package. His eyes are half-mast while my fingers slowly creep up his thighs.

He doesn't flinch, but I can feel his cock bobbing up and down with excitement.

And I can't help wonder how big it is. How much harder it can get. How long ago it's been.

So I hook my fingers underneath his boxershorts and tug them down.

He doesn't stop me.

I marvel at the sight of his massive cock as its released from its prison, fully glistening with pre-cum.

I lower myself between his legs and open my mouth, hovering closer to him with my tongue dipped out until it touches his shaft, and fuck me, the explosion of lust in his eyes is nearly enough to make me come.

He strains against the chair while I circle my tongue around. "Kayla … Please."

"Please … what?" I murmur, as I take him into my mouth and begin to suck. "Stop?"

He sucks on his bottom lip again as I roll my

tongue over the tip, and with a cracked voice he begs, "More."

A grin spreads on my face as I dip down further and further until I hit the base of his cock and a long-drawn out, almost desperate moan leaves his mouth.

"Fuck," he grits.

His length throbs in the back of my throat, and I pull out to take a breath, only for him to grab my curls and shove my face right back onto his dick.

"You're too good for me," he murmurs, his head tilting back once again as I lick his shaft. "Oh, fuck me, your tongue is divine," he groans.

I pull out to breathe and look up into his unfathomable eyes. "Thank you … Sir."

His eyes flicker with greed, and his hand reaches for my face, caressing my cheek so softly I melt into the palm of his hand. "Say that again."

"Thank you, Sir."

His dick bobs up and down against my breasts. "I can't fucking resist you."

When I try to go back down again, he keeps me steady just by my chin and he actually manages to lift me up with just one finger alone. As I come to a stand, his other hand grabs my thigh, pulling me between his legs. His hand slowly slides up my inner thigh, pushing the fabric of my leggings into my pussy as he starts to rub me. It's hard not to moan while he expertly circles around and around, his gaze never failing to hold mine.

Quietly, observantly, we've been descending into obsession without anyone ever noticing.

Unable to hold it back any longer.

RIP!

With just one tug, he's managed to pull down my leggings, exposing my thin, see-through thong, which he rips apart with ease.

He grabs my waist and lifts me onto his lap, where we stay for a moment, basking in each other's presence. And I can't help but peer into those dark, wistful eyes filled with so much desperation and unfathomable pain that it momentarily takes my breath.

"Do you want this?" he asks.

I nod.

"Say it."

"I want you to fuck me."

His hands slowly run down my ass, feeling me up, before he lowers me onto his cock, which is hard as a rock. I can feel every pulse of his veins as he enters me slowly, deeply, as if to savor the moment before it disappears.

As he buries himself inside me to the hilt, he groans, and my body erupts with goosebumps.

God, he feels so fucking good inside me.

Even though I know I wasn't supposed to do this.

Even though I know he's the dean.

Someone much, much older than I am … I want him, right here, right now.

He tips down my chin and brushes his lips past mine, cooly observing me from his chair before he gently presses them onto mine, stealing a silky-smooth kiss from my full lips.

Right then, he pulls out only to thrust back in so hard I moan loudly into his mouth. A wide, cocky grin spreads on his lips as he repeats the same motion with the same effect, causing me to ripple in and out of madness with each of his strokes, his cock filling me up and then some. His kisses are both soft and crude, ravenous, like he can't get enough and wants to remember how they feel at the same time.

I smile against his lips. "How long ago has it been?"

"Too long," he growls, thrusting in faster and faster, digging his fingers into my ass.

"I can tell."

"Can you now?"

He hooks his fingers underneath my shirt and pushes it up so fast I squeal when his mouth covers my nipple. He bites and tugs as he thrusts into me deeply. "I almost forgot how good it could be."

He lifts me up and pushes me back down over the head of his cock, spreading my wetness all over as he lavishly licks both my nipples like he hasn't touched any in years. I tilt my head back and grab his hand, bringing it up to my neck.

"Oh … you like being choked, huh?"

His fingers automatically squeeze on just the right spot, making stars dance in my eyes, and my pussy clenches with need.

"Fuck," I groan.

"Yes, that's it. Make that sound. Moan for me."

I moan louder as he thrusts in even harder, while one hand squeezes off my jugulars and the other firmly digs into my skin.

"Are you going to lose your breath for me?"

I can't speak, can't even think about anything other than how good it feels to be riding this man's dick.

The moment he releases me from his grip, I suck in a breath, and he whispers into my ear, "First you're going to make me come inside that eager pussy of yours, aren't you?"

"Tease," I murmur.

As if it's a form of punishment for talking back, he impales me on his cock and bites into my lip, before kissing me so deeply I melt into a puddle right on his lap. He moans into my mouth and spears me with his tongue, forcing me to feel him everywhere.

"Fuck, you make me want to fill you up," he groans.

"Say please again and I might let you."

He tears into me and buries himself inside me to the base before whispering against my lips, "Please … let me come inside this perfect pussy."

I moan as his balls squeeze together against my thighs. "Oh, yes."

His eyes nearly roll into the back of his head as all his muscles clench and his cock empties itself inside me. Warm cum streams down from my pussy as he continues to pump into me until he's sated.

But within seconds, he stands up and puts me down onto his desk, shoving all his papers off, then splays his fingers across my chest to push me all the way down.

"What are you doing?" I ask. "You already finished."

"But you haven't," he says. "Now let me have a taste of the divine."

The moment his tongue hits my clit, I nearly lose it. My head buckles back against the wood as my legs yield to his strong grip and that expert tongue swiveling back and forth across my pussy.

Good God, this man can lick like he's gotten a gold medal for it at the Olympics.

I've never felt anything this good in my life.

"Holy shit," I groan.

A low, rumbling laugh emanates from his chest, reverberating against my skin, causing delicious shockwaves. "You've only ever been licked by boys. Now let me show you how a real man eats his five star meal."

His tongue drives into my pussy, circling around, licking every inch he can reach until I'm shaking on his desk. My nails dig into the wood as he rolls his tongue around my clit and kisses my mound like he's enjoying his dinner.

Fuck, this is going to make me come so fast, I am not prepared.

"That's it, show me what you look like when you come for me," he groans.

My moans become louder and louder, his dirty words sending me over the moon and back.

I'm not ready, it's too quick, I shouldn't be doing this, oh God.

Too late.

A loud moan rolls off my tongue as his rolls around my clit and delicious shockwaves fill my body with ecstasy. My eyes nearly roll into the back of my skull as he keeps licking me all the way through the orgasm, lapping up the juices and cum with delight.

And when I've finally come down from the high, my legs feel like they've turned to mush.

He helps me up and I hold onto his shoulders to steady myself before I lean in and kiss him on the lips. Every kiss is returned with an equally needy kiss … and lingering doubt. But if I keep my eyes closed the world will fade and maybe we can stay like this for a little longer.

His lips part against mine. "We shouldn't have done this."

"We definitely shouldn't have," I mutter.

When my eyes open again, his are filled with regret. The dean … in shock.

Oh God.

What have I done?

I clear my throat and let him go, then jump off the desk, as he tucks his dick back inside.

"I'm sorry," I mutter to myself as I pull my leggings back up and put my shirt down. "I don't know what got into me. I—"

He grabs my arm and stops me mid-way through the room. "Don't be sorry about something we both needed." He gently smiles. "Once."

"Once," I repeat, telling myself it'll be enough. "Making a mistake *once* is enough."

His Adam's Apple goes up and down as his eyes linger on my body, my face, as if he's taking it all in at once. "I … wanted to thank you. For your help."

I nod. "Don't … mention it."

"I want you to know that I admire you, and I wish I could, but … I'm a scarred man, Kayla. I don't do relationships." He looks away for a moment and releases me from his grip. "It wouldn't be right."

"I understand," I say. "And also because I'm friends with your son and daughter."

"Exactly," he repeats, his voice unsteady.

I rub my lips together. "We just needed to fuck it out of our system. And that's it."

"Right," he says.

"Okay. Well, it was fun."

When I turn around again he adds, "I'm sorry. I wish it could be more. But I don't want you to be in danger."

I pause near the door. "I know. I promise I won't tell a soul. Not about the man you killed. Or what we did in here. But don't ever ask me to forget." I look him in the eye one last time, but the moment he takes a step towards me, I close the door behind me.

***

The next day

I take my earbuds out and stop jogging, right near the spot where Mr. Rivera killed that man. But there is no body. Not a speck of blood. Nothing left of the crime he committed. It's as if it never even happened.

But I know I didn't dream it up.

How did he clean up this body in a single day?

Even if I'd ask him, I doubt he'd tell me the truth. Not just because he doesn't want to, but because he's protecting his family. Because he wants to protect *me*.

I shudder and turn around again, jogging all the way

back to campus where the bustling school life almost makes me forget about what I've witnessed. Until I see him. Standing there with a cigarette in his hand, leaning against the side of the main building, wistfully staring off into the distance.

I wonder what he's thinking about.

If he dreamt about me last night like I did about him.

If he's already forgotten me.

That man … I could never forget someone like him.

I gulp and resume my jog all the way back to the sorority, where I shut the door and breathe in and out a few times. Until my breathing comes to a full stop. Because on the table, right next to the door, is a giant—and I mean giant—bouquet of flowers with my name on it.

I stare at it for a moment as I gather the courage to approach, but my curiosity is too big to ignore.

I pick up the note and open it up. I'm blushing so hard it feels like my head is going to explode along with my heart.

I knew you'd remember me. Don't ever forget or give up.

...

Good girl.

Yours,

Salvatore

THANK YOU FOR READING!

Thank you so much for reading MEN WHO YEARN. I hope you enjoyed. You could really help out by leaving a review. Thank you!

This story was a short prelude into **BOYS WHO HUNT**, a new Dark Bully RH/Why Choose Romance in the Spine Ridge University world.

Read on for an EXCERPT of BOYS WHO HUNT!

PROLOGUE

Ivy

"Where do you want your next cut, little thief?" Silas asks as the blade points at my chest, his purge mask haunting me.

Heath hovers over my face, his mask glowing in the dark, as he trails his finger down my body until he's right beneath my sternum. "Here?"

I shake my head.

Silas smiles as he points it at my legs. "No. Here …"

I gasp when the edge pierces my skin only briefly, causing one droplet of blood to cascade. He groans and leans over to lick it straight off my skin, and the hum that follows creates chills all over my body.

"Devilish little vixen," Silas whispers.

My brain has floated off into the unknown. Sweet, sweet nirvana … beyond destruction.

I still feel the burn on my skin right where he carved me… still feel the arousal building in my body with the need for more. More insanity.

"You love this, don't you?" Max says, spreading my legs apart.

I nod.

Even though I know these boys are wrong for me.

They're beyond filthy and out of their minds insane.

But I still want them anyway.

I was a runner, an escapee, fleeing from my past, fleeing from the present.

I ran so fast my legs could barely carry me until they started chasing me … and carried me instead.

They caught my body and used it as they saw fit, chaining my heart and soul to their unhinged ways. I've fallen into their dark pit of desires and don't want to crawl back out. Not even if it kills me.

Heath slowly zips down above me. "Who do you belong to?"

"You. All of you," I murmur.

"Then you're going to be a good little slut and beg for us," Heath groans.

My entire body shivers as both he and Max touch me everywhere, hands creeping underneath my blouse, into my pants, all over my body.

They've distorted my mind beyond comprehension and wrecked my heart until all it wanted was the taste of the hedonistic freedom they offered me.

And I realize now I'm not the only thief. I never was.

These boys have seized all the dark fragments of my soul, and I never want them back.

A devious grin spreads on Silas's lips as he crawls

on top of me, hovering dangerously close, and he sucks in a breath. "God, you smell so good when you're scared, my pretty little thief," he whispers into my ear, his tongue darting out to lick the rim. "Now run."

ONE

Ivy

Nothing is more priceless than the smug faces of rich boys who think they're untouchable ... just before I've robbed them.

I walk around through the dark, wood-paneled halls of the Skull and Serpent Society, amazed at the wealth on display. Century-old paintings and extravagant statues are covered in drinks and food while masked people dance away to the loud music blasting across the giant mansion, believing they'll stay anonymous. Safe.

But what draws my attention the most are three boys on the expensive leather couch in the back of the common room, drinking liquor straight from the bottle, all wearing LED purge masks that strike terror into the hearts of anyone who even dares to glance at them.

I've been at Spine Ridge University long enough to know exactly who to avoid.

These boys are at the top of my list.

The one on the left—a tall, muscular guy with a piercing in his lip and brow and tattoos all over—casually leans back into the couch as he takes a whiff of his cigarette right through the mask, his painted brown, medium-length hair loosely tucked into a bun, along with those black ear tunnels giving away who he is—Heath Preston, a notorious heartbreaker of Spine Ridge University, and the eldest of the three.

The one on the right, with his lanky but muscular

frame and dark-brown hair swooping above his mask has a girl on his lap who's suckling on his knife earring, but his head is tilted over the couch and his eyes are fixated on Heath as he bites his lip. Max Fletcher is the youngest of the boys, an eternal dreamer, and definitely the odd one in the crowd.

But the one that really makes all the hairs on the back of my neck stand up is the one in the middle. The shortest of the three, but the one who's the most fucked up—Silas Rivera.

He flashes the expensive bottle of liquor, running his fingers through his black tipped car-length hair and white roots, the little heart-shaped tattoo on his face a stark paradox to the piercing green eyes that flicker through the mask with deadly precision as he aims the bottle at a guest's head and chucks it at him.

The guest jumps aside, and the bottle smashes into a million pieces against the wall.

"No one said Phantoms were welcome tonight!" Silas yells.

The guy runs off through the crowd, and I step aside just in time for him to bolt through the door, leaving a cold gust of wind in his wake.

Silas Rivera laughs maniacally as the guy runs off, and the other partygoers laugh their asses off like it's one big joke. He runs his fingers through his hair and sits back down as a girl approaches him from the side with a box of bonbons in her hand.

"Aw … Cutiepie's getting a box of chocolates." Heath chuckles, shoving his elbow into Silas's ribs.

Silas looks at Heath like he's about to chop his head off.

"For your birthday," the girl says, blushing hard as she barely manages to glance at Silas.

Silas breaks out into a full grin, which reminds me of the Joker, the right edge of his full lips touching the heart-shaped tattoo on his cheek.

Suddenly, he grips her by the throat. "Chocolates. That's what you bring me?"

He snatches them from her hand and chucks them at Max, whose girl stumbles off him like she's scrambling to save her own life.

The noise in the room slowly dies down as they all focus on Silas and his tough grip on the girl's throat.

"I … I …" she mutters.

"What?" He leans in with a wicked smile on his face. "Say it."

"I like you."

"You *like* me?" The laughter emanating from his throat is nothing short of ominous. "Get on your knees for me, then."

The girl is slowly pushed down by the sheer force of his fingers squeezing the life out of her neck. I clutch the doorjamb with all the power I have to stop myself from intervening as a knife is flicked around.

He points it right at her face. "Do you like me enough to bleed for me?"

Her pupils dilate. "What?"

Heath leans forward too now, intrigued by the scene Silas is causing. "It's his birthday. Don't want to disappoint the birthday boy, do you?"

Silas holds the knife under her chin, and tears well up in her eyes as he slowly brings it to her lips. The whole room has gone deadly quiet. Even the music has died down.

"Do you want to make me happy?"

She nods.

The vicious smirk disappears. "Open your mouth."

She slowly parts her lips as tears roll down her cheeks. He inserts the knife, lays it on her tongue …

And then the grin on his face reappears as a fucked-up laugh follows.

He retracts the knife and releases her throat by shoving her away, causing confusion all around.

"Get out. You're not worth my time."

After a quick knife flip, he tucks it back into his pocket as the girl crawls away.

"Fuck you," she mutters as she scrambles to her feet. "Asshole."

"She doesn't seem to like you anymore," Max says, ogling her as she scurries off. Then he chucks one of the chocolates into his mouth.

Silas snarls, "Good."

I grip her wrist as she passes me. "Are you okay?"

She wipes the tear stains off her face and jerks her arm free. "I don't need your pity. Thanks."

She bolts off to the exit, and I understand why. Not only did she get humiliated in front of an entire crowd but he also scared the living shit out of her.

For a second there, I almost believed he was going to cut her, just like everyone here. He had us on the edge of our seats, wondering how far he would go and whether he'd finally veer off the dangerous tightrope he'd been walking all along. Always looking for the next hit to keep him smiling while surrounded by all that money can buy. But all the riches in the world couldn't fill the void these boys have in their hearts.

"Music, hello?" Heath growls, and within seconds, the music booms through the room again, drowning out the silence.

I take a last swig of my drink before I waltz out of the dance room.

I've made my decision.

Fuck these boys. They deserve everything coming for them.

I head into the bathroom and lock myself inside before I take off my bag and pull out a hoodie and black surgical mask, covering everything until only my eyes are visible. I open the door and look around again to make sure no one watches me as I head up the stairs.

The people attending the party are too busy dancing and chatting to notice me going into the hallway upstairs.

I rummage every room until I find one that's unlocked and not occupied by people having sex, and I head inside. Books line the walls of this room, and the bed in the back seems unkempt. The scent of burnt incense meets my nostrils as I head toward the closet and open every drawer, searching through the clothes. Boxers, black pants, black shirts with skulls and spiders on them, studded belts and necklaces. This must be Heath's room.

I get to the next closet and throw everything out until I find a very expensive-looking box from Cartier. "Well, hello there," I murmur, tucking it into my bag.

I check the rest of the closet, but there's not much else, and I'm definitely not getting the shoes, no matter how expensive they might be.

I open up some more drawers for some leftover dollar bills as well as an actual new, unused phone. Who keeps a phone carelessly in a box like it's a fidget and not a whole goddamn phone that probably cost a thousand bucks?

I doubt he even bought this himself.

Men are rich … but boys? Boys don't deserve the wealth they've been handed on a silver platter by their loaded parents. They don't even pay for their admission to this university. Silas's mom and dad own the RIVERA clubs across the globe, and his dad is the dean at this fucking college. The parents of these boys bought their spots long ago, while the rest of us have to work our entire lives to earn a scholarship to such a prestigious university.

I stuff the phone box into my pocket before I head to the room right next door.

A ton of skulls are all over the place like someone started a collection, and I don't know whether they're real, but I don't have enough time to care either.

I grab the wallet on the desk, fish out all the credit cards and bills until it's empty, then snag some rings from the top drawer. Then I filter through his closets, opening up a box in the back that makes my eyes almost bulge out of my head.

"Money shot," I murmur. There are stacks and

stacks of dollar bills, hundreds of them, maybe thousands.

And now they're all mine.

I take the whole box out and empty it into my bag, which is starting to feel heavy. Then I look around the room and underneath the bed, where I find a particularly strange little box. The lid is closed, but it's easy to break into as it looks like one of those boxes kids use to hide stuff in. I crack it open with one of my smaller keys, hoping to find some interesting loot.

Instead, there's a shiny, plastic red flower inside.

Why is he keeping this in a box?

CREAK!

The sudden noise makes me stop and look up.

What was that?

It sounded like … footsteps.

Panic bubbles to the surface.

Shit!

With the box still in my hands, I bolt out of the room, but the second I spot Silas's black-and-white hair and those eerie tats running all up the back of his neck as he walks up the stairs, I immediately go back inside and shut the door, holding my breath.

Shit. What the hell do I do?

I check the room and find two windows in the back. One is bolted shut, but the other is opened a little bit.

Can I fit through that?

Silas's footsteps make the wooden floor creak.

There's no time.

Without thinking, I tuck the little box in my bag and run to the other end of the room. With all my strength, I push open the window and slip through, one leg after the other, squeezing my body through the narrow gap, ripping my bag half open at the zipper from the hook on the window.

"Goddammit," I hiss, pulling it through as I land on the balcony.

"What the fuck?!"

Silas's deadly voice makes all the hairs on the back of my neck stand up.

Guess he found the mess I left.

I look over the balcony, but there's no way to go down except a big-ass tree in front of the house.

Should I risk it?

"Whoever's in my room, you're dead if I catch you!" Silas's loud growl is all I need to make the jump.

I grab the tree's branches and catch myself just before falling, but fuck me, my heart's shooting through the roof. This stuff had better be worth it.

I grasp the tree trunk and make my way down each branch, but one of them gives way underneath me, and I tumble to the ground, knocking me out for two seconds.

My head is spinning.

I can't hear from one ear.

I swiftly search my way around the grass, but it's hard to see in the dark.

Shit. Shit. Shit! I don't have time for this.

A door is loudly thrown open mere feet away from me.

Fuck. I have to run.

Without looking, I scramble to my feet and run in the opposite direction with a half-broken bag and a few stray bills flying left and right like a trail left by Hansel and Gretel.

ALSO BY CLARISSA WILD

Dark Romance

Debts & Vengeance Series

Dellucci Mafia Duet

The Debt Duet

Savage Men Series

Delirious Series

Indecent Games Series

The Company Series

FATHER

New Adult Romance

Fierce Series

Blissful Series

Ruin

Rowdy Boy & Cruel Boy

Erotic Romance

The Billionaire's Bet Series

Enflamed Series

Unprofessional Bad Boys Series

Visit Clarissa Wild's website for current titles.

www.clarissawild.com

ABOUT THE AUTHOR

Clarissa Wild is a New York Times & USA Today Bestselling author of Dark Romance and Contemporary Romance novels. She is an avid reader and writer of swoony stories about dangerous men and feisty women. Her other loves include her hilarious husband, her cutie pie son, her two crazy but cute dogs, and her ninja cat that sometimes thinks he's a dog too. In her free time, she enjoys watching all sorts of movies, playing video games, reading tons of books, and cooking her favorite meals.

Want to be informed of new releases and special offers? Sign up for Clarissa Wild's newsletter on her website www.clarissawild.com.

Stay up to date of new books via Clarissa's website: www.clarissawild.com

You can also join the Fan Club: www.facebook.com/groups/FanClubClarissaWild and talk with other readers!